The Adventu...

Seek and Save

LOST IN THE DARK

Written by Sharon Swanepoel

Author: Sharon Swanepoel

Illustrator: Lucas Loscinto

Layout and design: Rudi Swanepoel

Dedicated to all still need to hear the Good News!

P. O. Box 1430, Dacula, GA 30019. / www.SeekandSave.us
Printed in China

Hi, I am Tell, and I am going to tell you a story,
so listen well.

Get ready to hear yet another adventure of Seek and Save.
You will hear the story of Tom who is stuck in a cave.
While John goes to find help for his friend,
he has no idea of the danger just around the bend

The Adventure Troopers were setting up camp,
Tom and John were bored.
They just could not wait any more, it was time to explore.

John's excitement began to show.
He was trembling from head to toe!
They saw a huge dragonfly darting to and fro.
Together they cried out, "Let's go!"
Troop Leader Tell had issued a warning earlier that morning.
He said, "Boys, do not try to explore on your own.
These woods are too dangerous to roam alone."

There were rumors that a mountain lion was seen nearby. The two boys ran deeper into the woods chasing the big dragonfly.

Oh the trill of adventure and danger.
This adventure however, would be a life-changer.
Tom had red hair, freckles and his friends called him Chubby.
He was exploring with John, his best buddy.
John was tall, skinny and his hair was kind of fuzzy.
He had big brown eyes and his shoes were always muddy.

Tom and his pal had lost track of time.
While back at the camp, Tell was calling an assembly line.
As John and Tom's names were called
it was obvious they were not there.
James saw them two hours ago when he asked for some candy
but they would not share.

Tell started a search for the boys at Crazy Bear Camp.
The boys were nowhere to be found;
they even searched under the boat ramp.

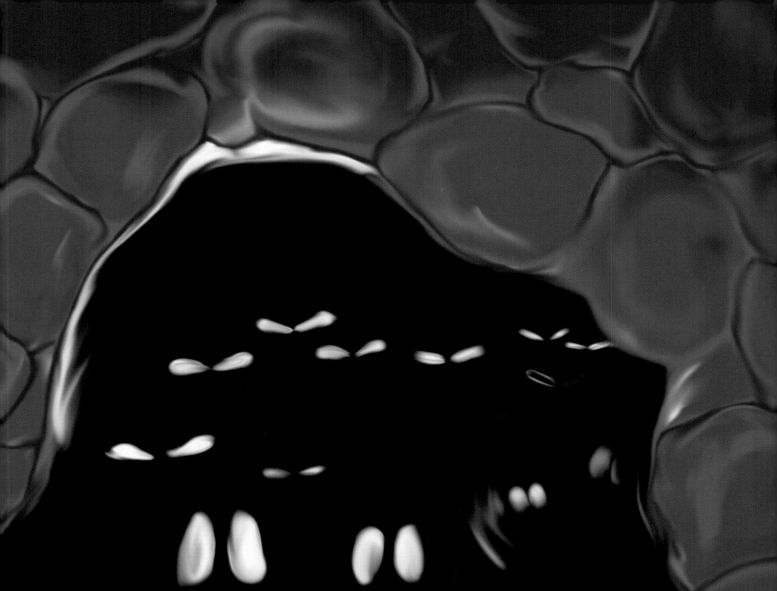

All the while, Tom and John were trying to find their way back,
when it started to rain.
They tried to remember which path to go,
without a compass all the paths looked the same.
Deeper and deeper into the woods they roamed.
It started to get dark and twilight glowed.

They saw a cave and entered in to get shelter from the rain.
Inside the cave they saw big glowing eyes and their legs went
lame.
They were so afraid,
"HOOT, HOOT, HOOT" was the sound it made.
Wha. . . What could it be?
Tom shone his flashlight better to see.

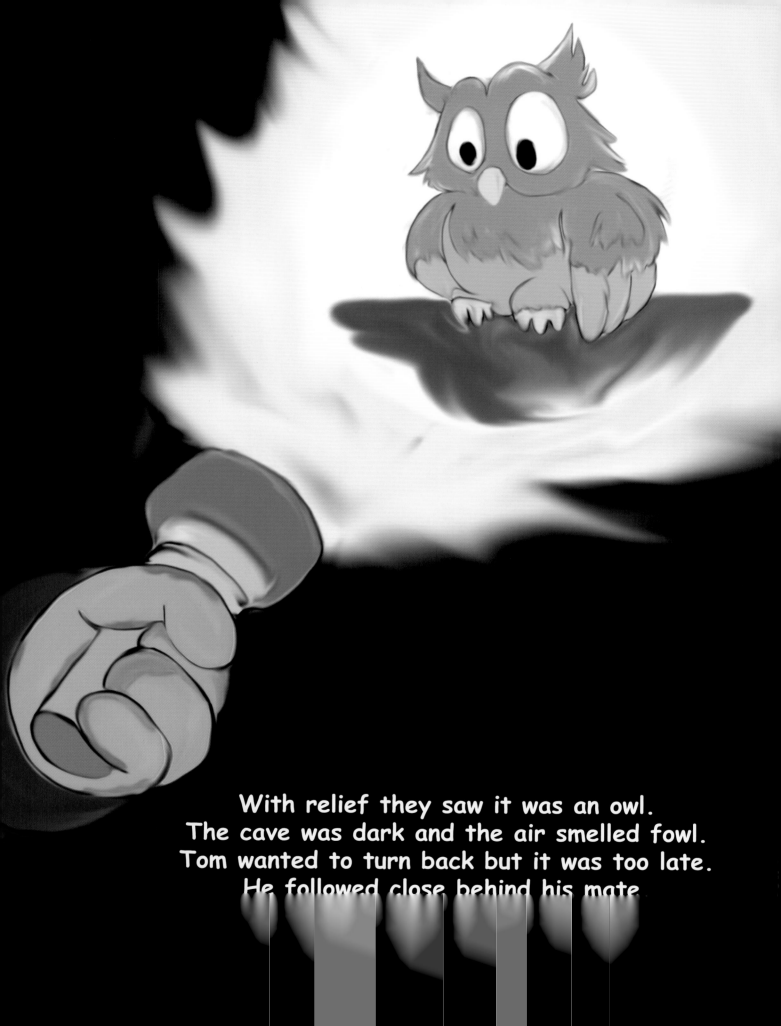

With relief they saw it was an owl.
The cave was dark and the air smelled fowl.
Tom wanted to turn back but it was too late.
He followed close behind his mate.

Deeper into the cave they wandered breathing in the damp air.
What happened next turned into a nightmare.

There was a rumbling and a falling of rocks.
The cave wall tumbled down like building blocks.
Tom had his foot caught under a huge rock.
He was trembling head to toe out of shock.

He shouted, "HELP!"
("Help" ... "Help" ...) came the echo.
Silence, then something moved.
He shone his light and saw a gecko.

John was stuck on the other side of the wall.
"Tom!" John cried out and Tom heard his faint call.
"Are you alright?" John muttered.
"Yes, but my foot is stuck under a rock."
Then he dropped his flashlight, loudly on the floor it clattered.
"Tom, I am going for help!", John stated.
Then from all the pain and distress, Tom fainted.

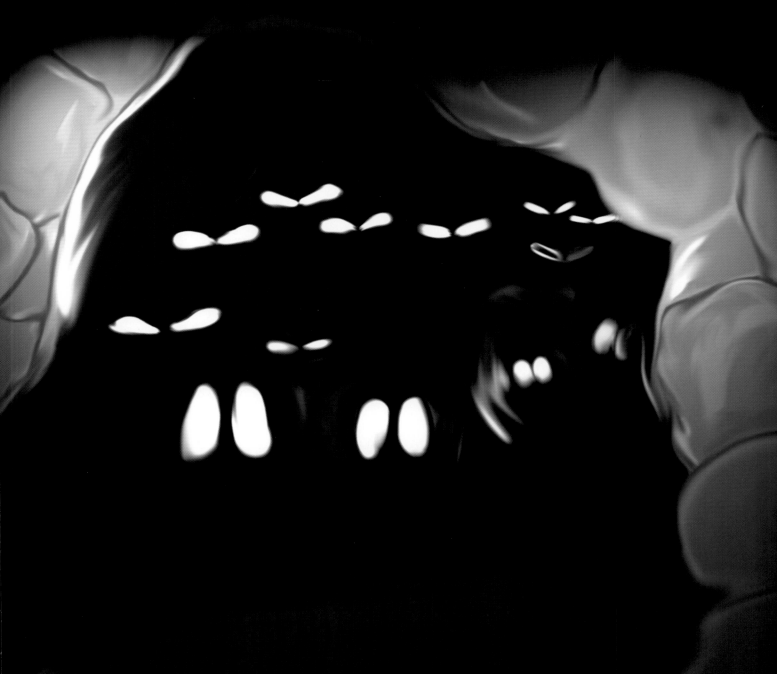

John made his way to the mouth of the cave.
Tom was in trouble, the situation looked grave.
John reached the mouth of the cave, it was very dark.
In the distance he heard a mocking bird imitate a lark.

John stepped out of the cave into the night air.
Was it his imagination or was something moving over there?
His heart was beating like a drum,
his every muscle tighter than a drum's snare.
There is was again. . . something in the bushes moving slow.
He heard a growling sound; was that his tummy?
Lunch was a long time ago.
Squeaking bats entered the cave darting to and fro, catching
insects in midair, putting up quite a show.

John had no idea which direction to go.
North, South, East, or West, he just did not know.
He felt a shiver down his spine.
His hair stood erect like the quills of a porcupine!

John prayed a prayer, pinching his eyes shut tight,
he muttered, "Lord Jesus, please protect me through the night.
Keep me safe 'till morning light."

He was on his own in Crazy Bear Park,
lost and alone in the dark.
Why was it called Crazy Bear Park? He pondered.
Then Tom heard a growling sound from over yonder.

Seek heard a ring tone from his cell phone,
just as he was throwing his dog a bone.
His dog was named Snout.
Snout came running when Seek gave a shout, "Snout!"
The brown bristles of Snout's coat made him look like a billy goat
Save was on the hammock fast asleep.
"Ring, Ring!" Seek's phone impatiently bleeped.

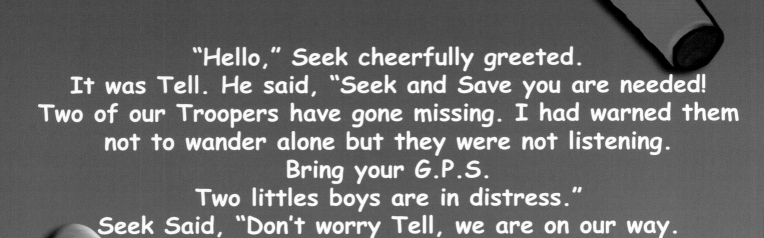

"Hello," Seek cheerfully greeted.
It was Tell. He said, "Seek and Save you are needed!
Two of our Troopers have gone missing. I had warned them
not to wander alone but they were not listening.
Bring your G.P.S.
Two littles boys are in distress."
Seek Said, "Don't worry Tell, we are on our way.
We will leave right away.

Seek and Save arrived at the camp.
It was dark so each of them carried a lamp.
Hastily from the camp they departed.
Their search for the boys had started.
The boy's tracks were not hidden from Seek's keen detection.
It was clear that the boys had gone in a northerly direction.

Seek's night vision goggles rested on his tummy.
Save had seen Seek wear them before
and he thought Seek looked funny.

Save sported a head band flashlight and his trusty rescue gear.
In the face of danger he showed no fear.
With the night vision goggles Seek could see
every muddy footprint left behind.
Seek and Save, on a brave new mission, the lost boys to find.

Up ahead Seek and Save could see a bridge.
It created a place to cross over the cavernous ridge.
The bridge had started to decay.
Just in time Save saw it and said, "Seek don't go that way!"

Shining in the moonlight beneath them they could see a river...
that's a long way to fall!
Seek felt his liver quiver! Oh, that was a close call.
Now they had to find an alternative route.
Seek leading and Save hot in pursuit,
for this was no time to wander about.

Seek and Save thrashed through the dense brush.
The leaves under their feet were a soggy mush.
Far away in the distance they heard a mountain lion roar.
The sound came from ahead and
they moved even swifter than before.
Seek looked through his goggles and saw a flash of light.
It was just a spark in the dark of night.
"Let us hurry!" Seek said. "Come on, straight ahead!"

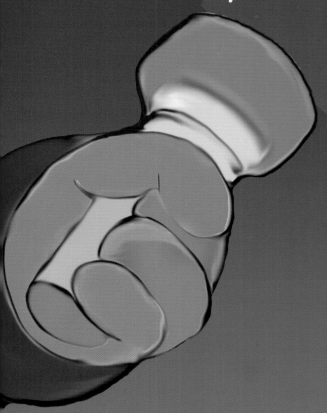

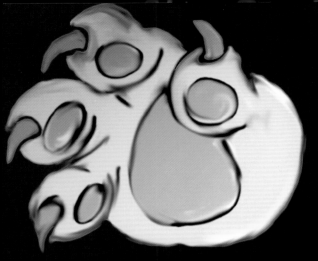

All the while in the dark John was alone
and he could feel eyes watching him.
He whistled a tune to hide all the fear within.
John reached down onto his pocket
and grabbed hold of the matchbox he knew was there.

As he lit the match he saw a mountain lion
just ahead, gazing at him in a hungry stare;
Eyes big a glowing in their sockets.
Then he saw the mountain lion retreat like a rocket.
The flash of his light scared off the lion
but John knew he would be back.
That lion was looking at him as one would look at a snack!

He had to build a fire to protect him through the night.
If the mountain lion comes again
he will drive him away with the fire's light.

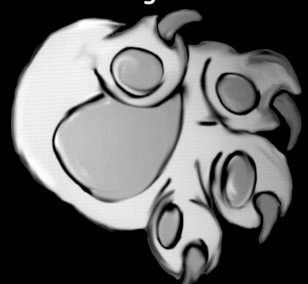

So in the mouth of the cave he built a fire.
He sat and watched as the flames grew higher and higher.
Suddenly out of the darkness the mountain lion appeared.
Glowing eyes, growing bigger and still bigger as he came near.
The mountain lion began to roar. . . "ROoAARR!"
John could not move, he was struck with dread and awe.

He thought this cannot be happening, it must be a dream.
Not knowing what else to do, John loudly let out a scream,
"HELP!"
Save leapt forward to get between John and the lion.
Trembling, from head to toe, John started crying.
Taking a burning log from the fire, Save drove the lion away.
"John, are you hurt?" Seek asked.
Sob. . .Sob. . . "No." John answered. "I am ok."

My friend, Tom is stuck in the cave and his foot is caught.
I tried to move some rocks away
but they are as sturdy as a fort.
I tried to go for help but my chances in the dark were naught."

Seek said, "Don't worry John, we have a special G.P.S.
It stands for: God's Power 2 Save.
It will not take us long to find your friend,
who is stuck in the cave.
With that said they entered the cave.
John was so thankful to have been rescued.
That was a close shave!

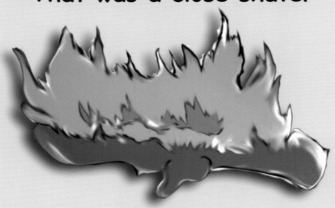

Back in the cave, Tom lay in the dark all alone and afraid.
This would never have happened, if they obeyed.
Oh, how he wished he had never left the camp.
He was so hungry and his clothes were damp.

If only Tom and John had heeded Tell's warning. . .
When will help arrive, will he have to wait 'till morning?
He just did not know.
Trapped in the dark all alone his fear began to grow.
His foot was stuck; he had no place to go.

Tears rolled down his cheeks, he was so scared.
Was that a creepy shadow he saw?
His vision in the darkness was impaired.
Tom remembered a song they had learned at Bible Camp.
He tried to remember the lesson Tell had taught them
about a lamp.

He sure could use one now in the dark.
Just then the song he had learned in him sparked.
The melody in his mind began to ring,
as Tom began to sing, he saw tiny flashes of light.
Fire flies were buzzing about. What a welcome sight!
Their buzzing made a harmonious sound.
Bottoms glowing, they buzzed all around
They happily "BUZZ" "BUZZ" BUZZED"
along as Tom sang his song.

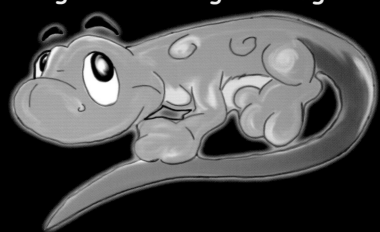

He sang:
"Jesus is the Light of the world
and He brings light into my heart.
Even if I'm lost, alone and in the dark,
from me He never will depart.
His word is a lamp to my feet.
I'm not alone, I'm in His keep.
So when I am afraid, I just call on Him and pray:
"Lord Jesus, come and light my way."
He will see me through. He knows just what to do.
Yes, Jesus is the Light; in His arms He'll hold me tight.
In the night He shines bright because Jesus is the Light."

Tom sang the song so strong that even a toad sang along!
"Rib-bet" Rib-bet"
Things moved all about the cave floor. "Jeepers Creepers"
Tom felt something move onto his new sneakers.
Then he felt something moving on his chest.
It started to hop beneath his vest.
"Rib-bet" "Rib-bet"
It seems Tom had found a friend in the cave.
If only his new friend would behave!
Tom remembered another song he had learned at camp.
F.R.O.G. the letter held the key:

F - Fully
R - Relying
O - On
G - God

So he sang the song called F.R.O.G.
F.R.O.G. . . Fully Relying On God I'll Be.
F.R.O.G. . . I Am In God's Company.
F.R.O.G. . . Even In The Dark I Can See.
F.R.O.G. . . In God's Care I'll Always Be.
F.R.O.G. . . Afraid I'm Not 'Cause God's With Me!

After singing he felt his courage grow. . .
He was cold and trembling from head to toe.
Tom tried to move his foot but it was still stuck.
He felt like a sitting duck.
Had something gone wrong?
Why was John taking so long?
So in the dark he just kept on singing the F.R.O.G. song. . .

Seek and Save entered the cave.
"Tom, Tom!" they kept calling out.
In the light of their lamps they could see critters scurrying about

Meanwhile Seek heard a voice echo in the cave.
Tom was singing. Seek said, "I can hear him, Save!"
Soon they saw the fallen rocks. They had found the site!
Save grabbed hold of a huge rock and heaved with all his might.
With every muscle flexed Save moved the rocks away
An opening appeared to their delight. HOORAY!

Seek looked through the opening made by Save.
OH, no! The situation looked grave!
Seek, with his night vision goggles on his head,
saw Tom lying in the dark just ahead.
Save saw the huge rock. Tom's foot was caught!
Save removed the rock and soon
Tom was freed by the strength he wrought.

Save picked up the boy
and carried him out of the cave into the cool night air.
John was so glad to see Tom,
he embraced him and ruffled his friend's red hair.

"It is time to go." Seek said.
"This cave is the mountain lion's lair.
She will be back soon so we need to take care."
They made their way back to camp, it was very late.
Both the boys were safe and their relief was great.

Holding onto John, Seek led the way.
While Save carried Tom, he said,"This has been quite a day."

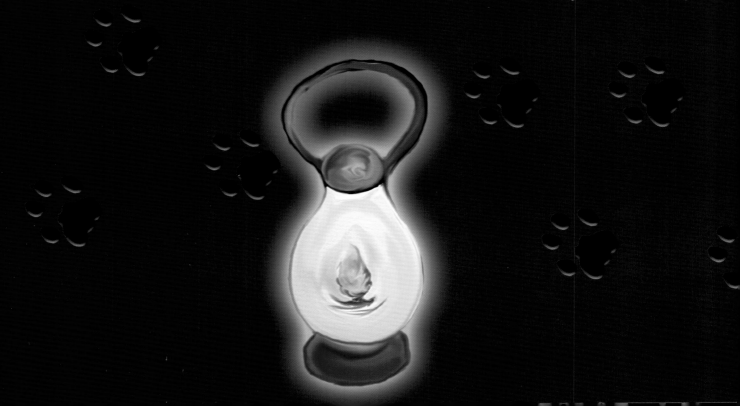

When they reached the camp,
they found Tell and the other troopers sitting
around the campfire.
They were so concerned about Tom and John
so to their tents they could not retire.
Tom and John, apologized to Tell for not listening.
They thanked Seek and Save for the rescue,
their eyes with tears were glistening.
The boys showed great regret,
this day they will never forget.

They sat by the campfire sharing their adventure with the rest
and told how their faith was put to the test.
Of God's faithfulness in the rescue, they were boasting,
while their marshmallows were toasting.

Tell said,
"Boys, this is what we can learn from this adventure today:
Be obedient and do not disobey.
Always listen to instructions given to you.
Obey your parents and your teachers too.
So, when you disobey and go astray,
pray, for in your darkest hour,
Jesus lights the way."

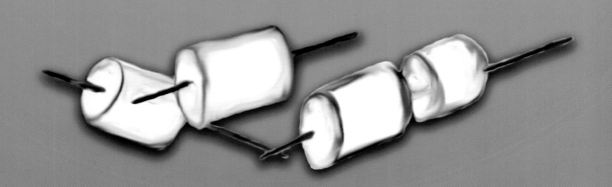

Satan goes around like a roaring lion seeking whom he may devour
Jesus will rescue you even in your darkest hour.
Call on Jesus, the Bible says His name is a strong tower.
Just like Tom,
we are stuck in our sin, with no way out.
Jesus will release us from our sin, fear and doubt.

Remember how Save rescued John from the mountain lion?
Satan too, like a roaring lion, might be on the attack.
You have no reason to fear because Jesus is near.
He will protect you, God has your back!

Jesus will rescue you; He has the power to save,
even though you are stuck in sin's cave.
The devil is no longer a threat.
Ask forgiveness for your sin and show regret.

Call on Jesus, just give it a shot.
In your sin Satan wants you to rot.
However, Jesus has uncovered Satan's evil plot.
Cry out to Jesus and make your decision.
He will rescue you with stealthy precision.

Jesus is the Light of the world.
It matters not if you are a boy or a girl.
The Bible says, "All of us have sinned."
So here is what you should do.
Pray this prayer of faith and God will save you:

Dear Jesus
I ask You to come into my heart today.
Come and wash all my guilt and sin away.
Forgive me that in sin I went astray.
Make me Your child this I pray.
Teach me to walk in You, the Way.
All my cares and burdens on You I lay.
Thank you for loving me in every way.
Guide me in Your will in all I do and say.
All this in Jesus' name I pray. AMEN.

John 8:12
"Then Jesus spoke again to them saying,
I am the Light of the world. He who follows Me shall not walk in
darkness, but shall have the light of life."

Isaiah 60:1
"Arise, shine; for your light has come,
and the glory of the LORD has risen on you."

Psalm 27:1
"The LORD is my light and salvation; whom shall I fear? The
LORD is the strength of my life; of whom shall I be afraid?"

1 Peter 5:8
"Be sober, be vigilant; because your adversary the devil walks
about like a roaring lion, seeking whom he may devour."

John 12:46
"I have come as a Light into the world,
so that whoever believes on Me should not remain in darkness."

Psalm 118:27
"God is the LORD, who gives us light."

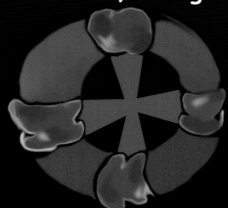

REMEMBER:
Jesus loves you and He came to seek and save you.

ACTIVITY CORNER

HELP TOM AND JOHN FIND JESUS

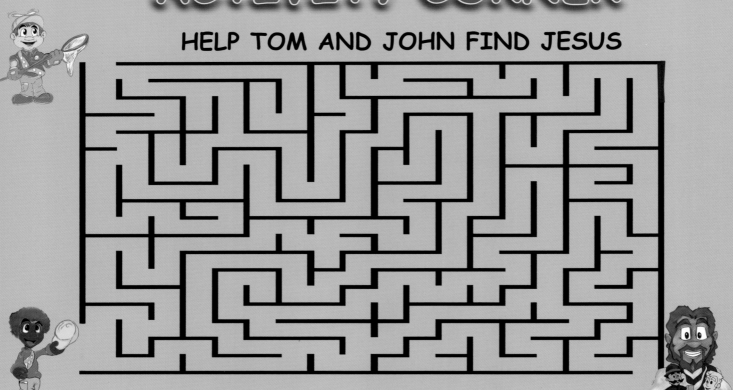

FINISH

||||||||||||||||||||||||||||||||||||||||||||||||||||||||||||||||||||||||||||||||||||||||

UNSCRAMBLE THE WORDS

1. ntianmou onil - _____ ____
2. ganord ylf - _____ ____
3. gihtl - _____
4. ravdentue - _____
5. mlleowsram - _____
6. yzarc reab prka - ___ ____ ____
7. thnig soivni gggesl -

____ _____ _____

WHICH IS DIFFERENT?
CAN YOU FIND THE PICTURE THAT IS DIFFERENT ?

Answer: 5

Answer:2

Answer:3

|||||||||||||||||||||||||||||||||||||||||||||||||||||||||||||||||||||||||||||

WORD SEARCH
LOCATE THE WORDS IN THE PUZZLE

C A N Y U T I M O N E Y J D F R E E T
L A T S T Y G V I N B G O P I J H G L O
S E A T V S E E K P A R U F A T F C V F
A V E F T V R S A D E R F S I N P E M
R E N H U J E S U S D E S A W R F R T
S M M H D E S T R O Y G F T F T G I H

1. SEEK   4. LOVE   7. TEA   10. SAD
2. SAVE   5. DESTROY   8. SIN   11. LOSE
3. JESUS   6. MONEY   9. FREE   12. SAW

QUIZ TIME
WITH TELL

QUESTIONS:
1. What were the boys chasing into the woods?
2. What was the name of the camp?
3. Who is the Light of the world?
4. What made the "HOOT, HOOT, HOOT" sound?
5. Who got stuck in the cave?
6. What made Seek look funny and rested on his tummy?
7. What entered the cave above John's head?
8. What did Tom see moving in the cave?
9. What is the name of Seek's dog?
10. What does F.R.O.G. stand for?
11. What roared in the distance?
12. Who goes around like a roaring lion?
13. Why did Tom and John get in trouble?
14. What did John do to protect him through the night?
15. What did Seek find that the boys left behind?
16. What did Save move to rescue Tom?

2. Crazy Bear Camp
3. Jesus
4. The owl
5. Tom
6. His night vision goggles
7. Bats
8. A gecko

10. Fully relying on God
11. A mountain lion
12. The devil
13. They did not obey
14. He prayed and built a fire
15. Muddy footprints
16. Rocks

Join
Seek and Save's
Team

Would you like to join Seek and Save
on a mission that Jesus gave?
Just like Seek and Save,
you can reach out to others too.
Read this scripture and you will know what to do:

And then He told them: "Go into all the world and preach the
Good News to everyone, everywhere."
Mark 16:15

You can rescue your friends just by telling them about Jesus.
Tell them that He loves us all and His love still frees us.
So whoever you are and wherever you may go;
to seek and save,
God's love you must show.
Do not stop at one,
let the whole world know
and the Kingdom of God will grow.

Take on this mission and you will see, part of Seek
and Save's adventure you will be. Reaching out for
your friends to see Jesus in you; a reality.

So show His love and say a prayer.
Jesus will be with you right there.
As you seek and save the lost.

PHOTO GALLERY

Children everywhere love the Seek & Save books!

Pictures taken in America, South Africa, Tanzania and Armenia.

SEEK AND SAVE

ADVENTURE MAP

COUNTRIES THAT SEEK AND SAVE HAVE BEEN TO:

2009-   Tbilisi, Republic of Georgia
2011 -   Tbilisi and Rustavi, Rep. of Georgia,
2011 -   Yerevan and Vanadzor, Armenia
2011 -   Western Cape, South Africa
2011 -   Gold Fields, South Africa
2012 -   Free State, South Africa
2013 -   Morogoro, Tanzania
2013 -   Cleveland, Ohio, USA
2013 -   Eau Claire, Wisconsin, USA
2013 -   Crowley, Louisiana, USA
2013 -   Western Cape, South Africa
2014 -   Huntsville, Alabama, USA
2014 -   Kwazulu-Natal, South Africa
2014 -   Western Cape, South Africa
2015 -   Williston, ND, Stanley, ND
2015 -   Boise, ID
2015 -   Musoma, Tanzania
2016 -   Mpumalanga, South Africa

(A total of 126,600 Seek & Save Books have been printed and distributed)

For more information about the Seek and Save Books and Project visit:
www.SeekandSave.us

www.facebook.com/SeekandSave.us

MORE SEEK AND SAVE BOOKS

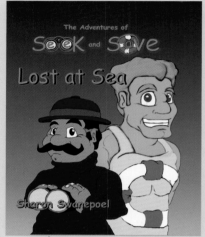

Lost at Sea

The Great Escape

The Village

For more information about the Seek & Save Books and Project
visit www.SeekandSave.us

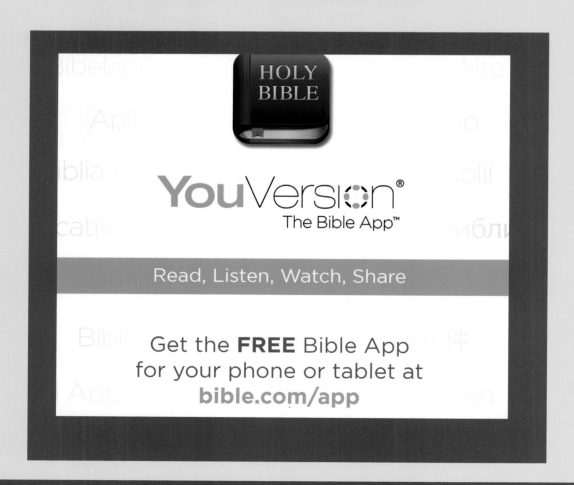